Summer in the Land of Anne

Story by Elizabeth R. Epperly
Illustrations by Carolyn M. Epperly

The Acorn Press
Charlottetown
Spring 2018

For our mother and father.

For Anne-Louise, Don, Marc, Jessica, and Mike, and for our grandchildren: Karlyn, Reid, Auguste, and Eleanor.

(ERE)

Gratitude to the beautiful models, my daughters: Caitrin Bridget Robinson, Keely Conlon Robinson, Ciara Epperly Robinson Lemery and Love to my granddaughter Liana Sullivan Lemery.

(CME)

"Mama, don't go!" wailed Elspeth. She threw herself against the front door with her arms stretched out.

Elspeth did not like her mother to leave the house without her. One time Elspeth hid in the back of the car. When her mother arrived at a meeting, Elspeth sat up and shouted, "Surprise!" Mama did not laugh. She drove all the way home again, and then she was late for work.

Willa, Elspeth's older sister, was disgusted with Elspeth for being so silly. Willa was always disgusted when Elspeth was silly. Elspeth adored Willa. Willa was eleven and Elspeth was six.

"Don't go!" Elspeth cried.

"Elspeth, dear, I'm going to the grocery store," said Mama.

Elspeth clung to the doorknob. "Why did you get out the suitcases?"

Mama smiled. "We're going on a vacation — all three of us. I'll tell you about it later. I have something special to read tonight."

"We're going on a vacation," Elspeth announced to Willa.

Willa was painting with watercolours. She made a yellow boat in a turquoise lake. Willa wanted to be a famous artist. "I know," she said.

"How come you know? Why doesn't anybody ever tell me anything?" said Elspeth in a loud voice.

Willa dipped her brush into the water glass. The yellow paint made the turquoise in the water turn green.

"Cool," said Elspeth, as she watched Willa twirl the brush in the new green.

Sounding as grown up as she could, Willa said, "I know because Mama told me. We're going to Canada."

Elspeth sighed. Willa knew everything. "What special thing is Mama going to read to us?" she asked at last.

This time Willa was surprised and looked at her little sister with interest. "I don't know. When's she coming home?" she asked eagerly.

Mama refused to answer questions. All through dinner, all through the evening, all through the brushing of their teeth and changing for bed, she would not tell them what she was going to read. She read to them every night, but had never made a secret of the choice.

Elspeth and Willa sat up in their green and purple twin beds, in their blue and white pyjamas, and their mother sat down in the chair between them. Lemon Drop gave one soft bark and then lay down at the foot of Elspeth's bed. He liked stories, too. Mama turned on the reading lamp and they saw the book on her lap.

"*Anne of Green Gables!* But Mama, I already know that story," Willa complained. "I saw the movie on TV last week!"

Elspeth hadn't watched the movie, but she had heard of *Anne of Green Gables*. Her best friend, Jenny, had a straw hat with red yarn braids attached. It was called an Anne hat.

"Is this about that red-haired girl?" asked Elspeth, pleased that Willa was pouting and she was not.

"Don't pretend you know about it, Elspeth!" cried Willa. "I know all about her! She was an orphan and she went to Prince Edward Island and she had red hair. Hey!" Willa suddenly stopped. "Is that where we're going in Canada — to Prince Edward Island? Because of Anne?"

Mama opened the book at chapter one and started to read. Listening, Elspeth felt she was floating on a laughing brook and waving to people she already knew: gossipy Mrs. Lynde and stern Marilla and shy Matthew. Finally she met Anne. She never heard anybody talk so fast!

When her mother kissed her goodnight, Elspeth whispered, "My real name is Anne."

It was a beautiful trip. They drove to Washington, D.C., and up through the New England states of New York and Connecticut and Massachusetts and New Hampshire and Maine. They crossed into Canada and drove through the provinces of New Brunswick and Nova Scotia. Mama wanted to take the ferry to PEI rather than the bridge. All through New England, Elspeth secretly planned what she would do on the ferry ride. Mama said the ferry would take a little more than an hour to go from Caribou, Nova Scotia, to Wood Islands, PEI. That was just the right amount of time for Elspeth. She had packed a plastic bag with her surprise in it.

Mama and Willa and Elspeth stood at the white railing and watched the water swirl around the ship.

"Look at all the kinds of blue!" said Willa, pointing at the deep blue summer sky and the rippling water and then at the purplish blue haze on the horizon that Mama said was Prince Edward Island.

"Mama, could I go to the bathroom, please?" whispered Elspeth. "It's right over there. Willa doesn't need to come."

Mama answered dreamily, staring at the sparkling water, "Yes, but don't be long."

Elspeth hugged her plastic bag and ran to the women's washroom. Here it was: the straw hat with red braids that Jenny had loaned her. Elspeth put on the hat, carefully pulling the elastic band under her chin. She stood on a chair in front of the long mirror and smoothed the red yarn braids and bangs. Two women smiled at her in the mirror.

"Why, Mildred, I believe we have Anne on board with us today. How do you do, Anne-spelled-with-an-e?"

Elspeth beamed and then said politely, "I'm fine, thank you, ma'am."

She wondered if Willa and Mama would recognize her — she felt so different.

Willa saw her first. "Oh, no! Mama, she's got that hat on! Please tell her to take it off. People are staring!"

Mama turned slowly and looked down at Elspeth. "Why, Willa, look! Here is Anne coming to join us on the trip over to the Island. How are you feeling today, Anne? Is that your carpet bag I see? Is Mrs. Spencer going to take you over to the Cuthbert farm in Avonlea?"

Elspeth smiled happily at Mama and ignored Willa. The three of them leaned against the rail and felt the gentle spray from the water below. The red cliffs and bright green fields of Prince Edward Island grew closer and closer.

In Cavendish, at the house called Green Gables, Elspeth removed the hat with braids when she saw she was surrounded by a dozen little girls wearing the same hats. It was hard to be Anne when so many others were pretending to be her.

Mama told them about the woman who wrote *Anne of Green Gables*. She explained that Lucy Maud Montgomery had visited this farmhouse and that it was now made to look like the Green Gables from the book. Mama said people got confused and thought the house really was Anne's house.

Inside the house, Elspeth felt confused, too. It was so much like the book described. Anne's bedroom had apple blossom wallpaper. A brown dress with puffed sleeves hung on the closet door. They saw a broken slate and a very old carpet bag. Marilla's black lace shawl was spread out on her bed, and Matthew's tin of pipe tobacco sat on the bedside table of his downstairs bedroom.

Mama showed Elspeth and Willa a photograph of L. M. Montgomery. Elspeth gave up trying to figure out if this was really Anne's house or not. What did it matter, anyway? Elspeth knew she was Anne herself, and the house did feel familiar. She looked around at all the braids and straw hats and felt sorry the other little girls could only pretend to be Anne.

They walked down Lover's Lane and up through the Haunted Wood. It all felt like home to Elspeth.

Mama took them across the road to the Site of L. M. Montgomery's Cavendish Home. Elspeth wanted to be the first to see Montgomery's real house. She ran ahead, up a little red pathway under some old spruce and apple trees. "Mama!" Elspeth called back in alarm. "Mama, somebody stole the house!" Elspeth felt alone and frightened. There was no house, only a basement made of red sandstone. Her eyes stung.

"Mama! Who took it?"

Mama smiled and motioned Elspeth to come to her. With a hand on the shoulder of each girl, she explained: "The house was torn down a long time ago by Montgomery's uncle. But this is the real place where Montgomery grew up as a little girl and where she wrote *Anne of Green Gables*. Look at this old apple tree — it was alive when Montgomery lived here. She may have sat beside this very tree and listened to the birds singing and the wind ruffling the clover fields."

Looking at the empty cellar, Elspeth felt sad. She wished Lemon Drop was here. "She lost her home, Mama?"

"Well," said Mama, "she lost the house, and that did hurt her. But she could always imagine it. If you close your eyes, you can still see the house."

Elspeth and Willa closed their eyes and they could hear the birds singing and the wind ruffling the clover and grass. The air smelled sweet.

"I can see the house," whispered Elspeth. "Can you, Willa?"

"Yes," whispered Willa, touching her little sister's hand. "I can."

"Montgomery wrote about the things she loved best and so she never really lost them," said Mama.

Elspeth took a deep breath. "She wrote so she could keep things?"

"Yes," said Mama. "And because she wrote about the things and the people she loved, we can love them and keep them too."

They walked around the edge of the old cellar. Elspeth skipped and Willa smiled at her. At the far end, where the steps led down to the basement floor, an apron of red sandstone surrounded a square of grass.

"This must be where the kitchen stood!" Mama exclaimed.

They stepped onto the grass. "It was right here, right where we are standing this minute, that Montgomery started writing *Anne of Green Gables.*"

"Right here?" Elspeth asked. Her mother nodded.

Elspeth stood still for a long time while Mama and Willa walked to the well. She closed her eyes and smelled the clover and listened to the birds. She imagined Montgomery in the kitchen, writing.

I wonder how long it takes to write a story, thought Elspeth.

Suddenly, near Elspeth's feet, a little red-striped head poked up out of a tiny hole. Quickly it disappeared. There it was again! Chipmunks! A dozen little tails whisked in and out between the sandstones of the cellar. A whole village of red-haired chipmunks! Elspeth's heart sang. The cellar wasn't sad — it was alive! She knelt on the grass and watched the chipmunks until Mama and Willa called her away.

A few days later, after learning the songs from the Anne musical and walking sandy beaches and riding bikes down red paths, days filled with chowder and wildflowers and the bluest skies they had ever seen, Elspeth and Willa and Mama leaned against the white railing of the ferry. They watched the red cliffs and the bright green fields of Prince Edward Island grow smaller and smaller.

"It's like leaving home, isn't it?" Mama said.

Willa clutched her bag of paints and admired all the kinds of blue she could see in the water and sky. She looked at Elspeth and smiled. "And where is your straw hat, Anne Shirley?"

"Oh, I'm not Anne," said Elspeth, lifting her chin. "I'm Elspeth of Cavendish, the famous writer. I have an apple tree and chipmunks. I write about things I love so I can keep them forever."

Elspeth of Cavendish

AC🜚RNPRESS

P.O. Box 22024
Charlottetown, Prince Edward Island
C1A 9J2
acornpresscanada.com

Printed in Canada
Edited by Penelope Jackson
Designed by Matt Reid

Library and Archives Canada Cataloguing in Publication

Epperly, Elizabeth R., author
Summer in the land of Anne / Elizabeth Rollins Epperly;
illustrations by Carolyn Epperly.

Issued in print and electronic formats.
ISBN 978-1-77366-005-9 (hardcover).
--ISBN 978-1-77366-006-6 (PDF)

I. Epperly, Carolyn, illustrator II. Title.

PS8609.P69S86 2018   jC813'.6   C2018-901125-4
                                       C2018-901126-2

Canada

Canada Council   Conseil des Arts
for the Arts   du Canada

The publisher acknowledges the support of the Government of Canada, the Canada Council of the Arts and The Province of Prince Edwards Island.